A New Coat of Leaves

A Book about Accepting the Way We Look

Educational Technologies Limited

A Child's First Library of Values

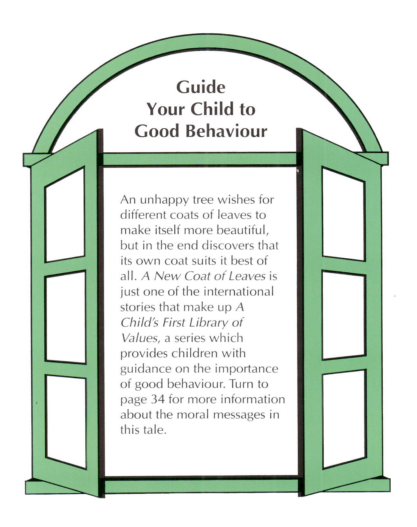

**Guide
Your Child to
Good Behaviour**

An unhappy tree wishes for different coats of leaves to make itself more beautiful, but in the end discovers that its own coat suits it best of all. *A New Coat of Leaves* is just one of the international stories that make up *A Child's First Library of Values*, a series which provides children with guidance on the importance of good behaviour. Turn to page 34 for more information about the moral messages in this tale.

story   place   forest

This story begins far, far away, in a very magical place. At the side of a lake, on the edge of a quiet green forest, there stands a beautiful little cedar tree. But the tree doesn't think it is beautiful. In fact, it is very unhappy with the way that it looks.

"The other trees all have beautiful leaves, but mine are small and pointed," says the tree sadly. "People prick their fingers on them and then they don't want to come near me."

"How I wish I could get rid of these sharp needles and have some smooth gold leaves," it wishes out loud. "Then everyone would like me."

✳ When the little cedar tree wakes up the next morning, it has a big surprise. Its wish has come true and it now wears a coat of beautiful golden leaves.

"How wonderful," thinks the tree. "Now everyone will admire my new coat of leaves."

It feels very proud of its glittering golden leaves.

✳ golden   ✳ wonderful   ✳ admire

✳ woodcutter   ✳ believe   ✳ precious

☀ When the local woodcutters see the tree they can't believe their eyes. They have never seen a tree with gold leaves before.

The woodcutters all want to take some of the precious golden leaves home. One by one, they pick the leaves, until the tree is left completely bare.

"Oh, my leaves," cries the tree, full of disappointment. "Perhaps I should have wished for glass leaves instead, then people would not want to take them away."

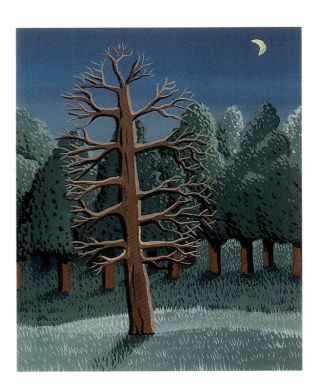

branch   delicate   wish

The following morning the tree has another surprise. Its branches are now covered with delicate glass leaves.

"Wow," thinks the tree. "My wish has come true again."

It is delighted with the shiny glass coat. But the animals grazing nearby don't even notice the change.

✳ shiny   ✳ nearby   ✳ change

✳ weather   ✳ suddenly   ✳ storm

Later that day, the weather changes suddenly and there is a bad storm. It rains heavily and strong winds howl through the forest.

The villagers are in such a hurry to get home that they don't even notice the little cedar tree. One by one, the delicate glass leaves are blown off by the wind and break on the ground.

Soon, not a single leaf is left on the tree.

"Oh no," wails the tree. "This was a terrible mistake. How I wish I had green leaves just like all the other trees around me."

wake   find   tender

Next morning, the cedar tree wakes to find it has a new coat of tender green leaves.

"Oh how wonderful," it says happily. "A beautiful coat of green leaves, just as I wanted."

It is sure that nothing can go wrong with these fine leaves as they move gently in the breeze.

✳ green ✳ breeze

❋ attention   ❋ a herd   ❋ goat

Soon the tree does begin to attract some attention. A herd of goats grazing nearby sees the tree with its tender green leaves. The goats begin to munch eagerly on the tasty leaves until not a single leaf is left. The cedar tree is bare once more.

That night, the tree is miserable again.

"Another disaster," it says sadly. "Maybe I should wish for something really different. Something to keep me warm, like a coat of feathers."

The following morning, the tree finds that its wish has come true once more. It is covered with pretty white feathers.

The tree sighs happily to itself.

But then it sees a huge flock of birds flying towards it. . .

❋ morning   ❋ once more   ❋ pretty

nest   beak   fly away

The birds want the feathers to line their nests. They each take a feather in their beak and fly away, leaving the tree bare once more.

The surrounding trees seem to be laughing, but the little cedar tree won't give up.

"Well, let me see," it thinks. "This time I shall wish for something that no one can take away. I wish for a coat of snow."

※ magic ※ fresh

✳ In the morning, the cedar tree is pleased to find that its wish has come true once again.

As if by magic, snow is falling over the cedar tree alone, and soon covers it in a coat of fresh white snow.

"Oh this is wonderful," it says. "I look gorgeous in my new white coat. This time it is sure to last."

But later that morning, the sun rises high in the sky and the snow begins to melt.

The local people are amazed to see the little tree covered in melting snow.

"It's magic!" they tell themselves.

The little cedar tree drips buckets of tears.

"I don't want to change any more," it says. "I feel so cold standing here naked again. I wish I had my own sharp needles back — at least they keep me warm."

✹ a sigh of relief   ✹ come true

The next morning, the tree is relieved to find that its wish has come true again and it is covered in its very own needle-like leaves.

Nearby, the other trees let out a sigh of relief.

"Our leaves are beautiful in the summer, but we lose them every winter and have only bare branches," they whisper. "You are lucky because your leaves stay green all year round. Be happy with your own leaves."

needle-like   summer   lucky

shelter ✸ at last ✸ feel

That winter, it snows heavily. Everything in the quiet forest is covered with a coat of thick white snow.

The cedar tree stands out from the other trees. Its branches and green needles make a good place for the birds and animals of the forest to shelter.

The tree feels contented at last.

"I'm happy to be a cedar tree," it says, "and I wish to stay just as I am. I will take good care of my needle leaves and be beautiful in my own natural way."

❋ happy   ❋ take good care of   ❋ natural

Do you remember?

Can you answer these questions without looking back at the story?

1. The cedar tree's own leaves are ...
   a. long and sharp
   b. long and smooth
   c. small and soft
   d. small and pointed

2. What happened to the cedar tree's delicate glass leaves?
   a. the woodcutters took them
   b. the villagers took them
   c. the wind blew them off the tree
   d. the birds broke them

3. Which coat of leaves did the goats like?
   a. the needle-like leaves
   b. the soft green leaves
   c. the gold leaves
   d. the glass leaves

4. Why do the other trees think the cedar tree is lucky?
   a. because it can change its leaves
   b. because its needles are pretty
   c. because its needles stay green all year round
   d. because it loses its leaves in winter

Do you know?

Look again at the story. Can you answer these questions?

1. Why is the cedar tree unhappy at the beginning of the story?

_____

_____

2. Why did the woodcutters take home the cedar tree's gold leaves?

_____

_____

3. Why was the cedar tree not happy with the white coat?

_____

_____

4. Why is the cedar tree happy with his green needle leaves at the end of the story?

_____

_____

ANSWERS: 1. d. small and pointed   2. c. the wind blew them off the tree   3. b. the soft green leaves   4. c. because its needles stay green all year round

Let's plan a picnic

You are planning a picnic. Where will you have it and what kind of food will you take?
Write your ideas and draw the food in the basket below.

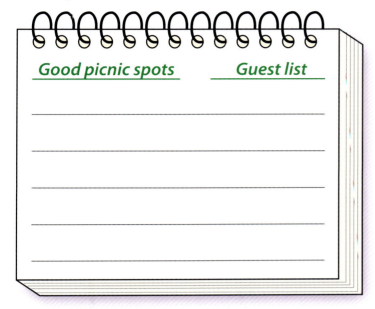

Good picnic spots   Guest list

Good picnic food

Spot the difference

Look at the pictures. There are 10 differences. Can you circle them?

Wordsearch

Can you find these words in the puzzle?
Hint: you can find the words by searching the grid from: top to bottom, left to right, right to left, or bottom to top.

cedar golden villagers
gorgeous needles precious
storm bare magical
leaves breeze sharp
beautiful delicate tender
snow glittering branches
feather woodcutter

```
O S J S T G B T G Y C M E U B
P S G E E O E Z M A G I C A L
H B D L N L A S U O E G R O G
N A A D D D U H U W E A O A W
S R R E E T A N I P I S R O
U E S E R N I R L H J J I A N
O W T N V F F P S E V A E L S
I W O O D C U T T E R I T I O
C J R N O H L B W P X B A Q H
E Z M Z S U R S M H Q R C T S
R Z R E H T A E F R D E I E F
P L Q B R A N C H E S E L I N
V I L L A G E R S G F Z E T Z
A G L I T T E R I N G E D B J
R A D E C G F F P R N Z Z K V
```

Write a sentence

Can you write a sentence using each of these words?

1. contented

_____

_____

2. wish

_____

_____

3. proud

_____

_____

Self Acceptance

Describe three things that the cedar tree learns by the end of the story.

1) _____

_____

_____

2) _____

_____

3) _____

_____

_____

Let's take a photo

Take a photograph of your favourite tree, and stick it onto the space below. Try to capture the character of the tree so that the photograph shows exactly what you like most about it.

What the story tells us. . .

- **Accepting the way we look.** Sometimes we don't feel happy with ourselves the way we are. We compare ourselves to other people and think that we are not as attractive, clever or interesting as them. In the story, the little cedar tree compares its own leaves to those of the trees around it. It thinks that it will be happier if it has different coats of leaves instead of its own needle-like ones. But the little tree tries many coats of leaves and eventually comes to realize that its own needles suit it better than any other leaves. In the same way, we should remember that we are all different and that sometimes those features that we see as disadvantageous are in fact our strong points. We should accept the way we look and learn to think positively about ourselves. As we become more positive, we will also feel happier and more confident.

- **Wanting others to like us.** In the story, the cedar tree tries to change its leaves so that it will become more likeable. It thinks that if it has a beautiful coat, then it will be more popular. But it is a mistake to think that people like us only because of our appearance and we should never try to change the way we look just to make ourselves fit in. People grow to like us because of who we are, not because of how we look. At the end of the story, the cedar tree discovers that the animals and birds of the forest do appreciate it just as it is and it doesn't have to try to look beautiful after all.

- **Being vain.** It is good to take pride in our appearance, but we should not be vain about the way we look. The cedar tree cares so much about the way it looks, that each time one of its smart new coats disappears, it is even more disappointed in its appearance. In the end, the little cedar tree learns to accept and like its own simple, natural looks.

A Child's First Library of Values
A New Coat of Leaves

Authorized English-language edition published by:
Educational Technologies Limited
A member of the Marshall Cavendish publishing group

First published 1997. New Edition 2017.
Printed in China.

Original story and illustration by Sophie Kniffke.
Sophie Kniffke was born in France in 1955. She graduated from Strasbourg University and won the grand prize at an international children's book exhibition in 1983.

Original Japanese-language edition published by:
Gakken Co. Ltd., Tokyo, Japan
© Sophie Kniffke/Minami Nishiuchi and Gakken Co. Ltd. 1992

ISBN-10: 0-7835-1314-3
ISBN-13: 978-0-7835-1314-0

www.ETLlearning.com